A Father's LOVE

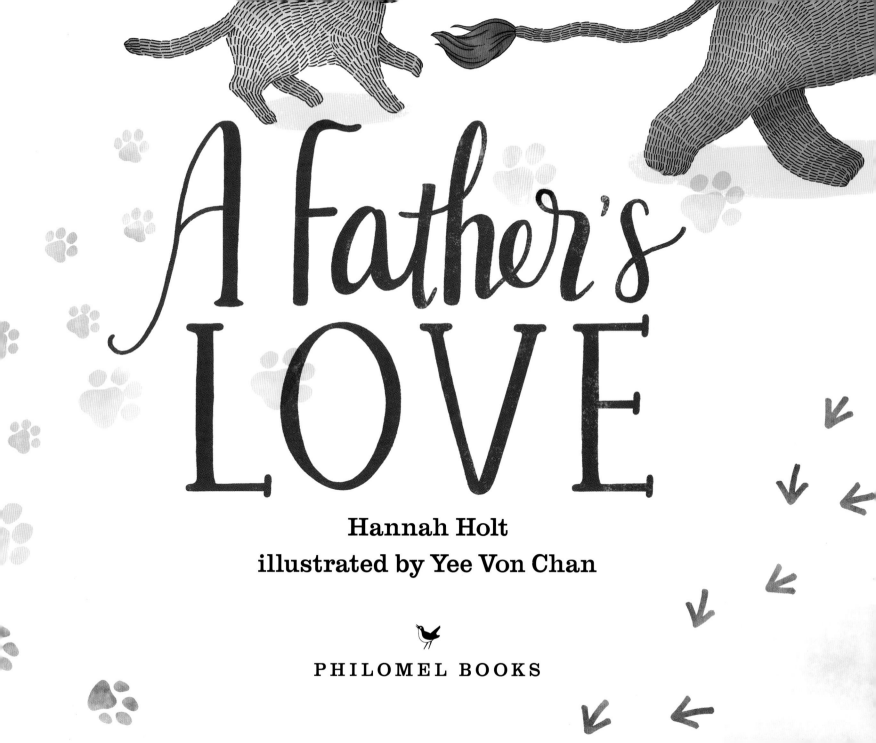

A Father's
LOVE

Hannah Holt
illustrated by Yee Von Chan

PHILOMEL BOOKS

Papas come in many stripes—
The big. The bold. The silent types.
Beneath the ground or high above,
each father's heart comes filled with love.

In swirling clouds of FROSTY WHITE,
a penguin snuggles baby tight.

He fluffs his down
from head to toe.
This father's love
is soft as snow.

Beneath a mighty REDWOOD TREE,
a fox tends to his family.

He keeps them safe
by digging chutes.
This father's love
runs deep as roots.

Riding through the PINK OF DAWN,
a tiny marmoset holds on.

Dad swings and plays
while on the run.
This father's love
shines like the sun.

Across a field of HAZY YELLOW,
this lion stalks a lazy fellow.

He charges Dad
with baby claws.
This father's love
has velvet paws.

A father toad dives quick, unseen
beneath a CREEKSIDE EVERGREEN.

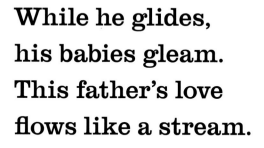

While he glides,
his babies gleam.
This father's love
flows like a stream.

A seahorse dad
protects his young
inside a pouch
until they're sprung.

His babies TWINKLE IN THE BLUE.
This father's love swims strong and true.

Nestled on a PURPLE LEDGE,
these baby falcons flap and fledge.

Their momma hunts.
Dad keeps them warm.
This father's love
soothes any storm.

The sky is dark—a PEPPERED GRAY—
but wolf cubs wrestle, yip, and play.

When Daddy howls,
they scamper in.
This father's love
rides on the wind.

For weeks and weeks, BROWN EMU sits.
Come hail or gale, he never quits.

He'll hatch them, raise them,
calm them—*hush*.
This father's love
is thick as brush.

Inside their homes, all WARM AND SNUG,
these dads and babies share a hug.

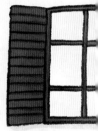

Kids fall asleep
with fingers curled.
A father's love
could hold the world.

A father's love is always there.

A father's love is . . .

. . . everywhere.

EMPEROR PENGUIN fathers keep their chicks warm by letting babies stand on their feet and huddling in groups with other fathers. They tend babies during the mothers' extended hunting trip to the ocean.

RED FOX fathers provide food and protection for the mother and her young kits. As the kits grow bigger, the father digs holes around the den and fills them with food to teach the babies how to sniff out meals.

PYGMY MARMOSET fathers carry their infants on their backs for several weeks. The babies need to nurse often, so the fathers will carry them to the mothers as needed.

LION fathers watch over cubs while the lionesses hunt. A lion father may even let the cubs play with his tail and mane.

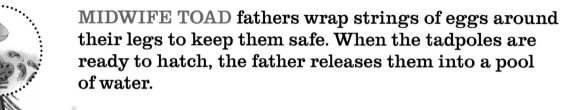

MIDWIFE TOAD fathers wrap strings of eggs around their legs to keep them safe. When the tadpoles are ready to hatch, the father releases them into a pool of water.

 **SEAHORSE** fathers carry their babies in a pouch until they are ready to be born. A father might give birth to 1,000 babies at once!

 **PEREGRINE FALCON** fathers help with keeping eggs warm and tending chicks. Falcons mate for life and will return to the same nesting place year after year.

 **GRAY WOLF** fathers provide food for both babies and mom while the pups are too young to leave the den. Once the pups are old enough to explore, the father's howl is used to call the family together and communicate over distances.

 **EMU** fathers build the nest, keep eggs warm, and raise chicks all by themselves. The father only rarely leaves the nest to eat or drink—losing 15 percent or more of his body weight while tending the eggs.

For Josh, who held our children through many long nights and who holds my heart forever. —H.H.

This book is dedicated to my father, whom I love and respect, and always lovingly supports my dream. —Y.C.

Philomel Books
an imprint of Penguin Random House LLC
Visit us at penguinrandomhouse.com

Text copyright © 2019 by Hannah Holt.
Illustrations copyright © 2019 by Yee Von Chan.
Penguin supports copyright. Copyright fuels creativity, encourages diverse voices, promotes free speech, and creates a vibrant culture. Thank you for buying an authorized edition of this book and for complying with copyright laws by not reproducing, scanning, or distributing any part of it in any form without permission. You are supporting writers and allowing Penguin to continue to publish books for every reader.

Philomel Books is a registered trademark of Penguin Random House LLC.

Library of Congress Cataloging-in-Publication Data
Names: Holt, Hannah, author. | Chan, Yee Von, illustrator.
Title: A father's love / Hannah Holt ; illustrated by Yee Von Chan.
Description: New York, NY : Philomel Books, [2019]
Summary: Throughout the animal kingdom and within snug houses, fathers express love for their children in their own unique ways. Includes facts about the animals featured.
Identifiers: LCCN 2018007929 | ISBN 9780525514206 (hardcover) | ISBN 9780525514237 (e-book)
Subjects: | CYAC: Father and child—Fiction. | Parental behavior in animals—Fiction. | Love—Fiction. | Animals—Fiction.
Classification: LCC PZ7.1.H6473 Fat 2019 | DDC [E]—dc23
LC record available at https://lccn.loc.gov/2018007929
Manufactured in China by RR Donnelley Asia Printing Solutions Ltd.
ISBN 9780525514206
Special Markets ISBN: 9780593203729 Not for resale
1 3 5 7 9 10 8 6 4 2

Edited by Jill Santopolo.
Design by Ellice M. Lee.
Text set in Clarendon.
The art was done in hand-drawn outlines with pencil & pen, then colored digitally.

This Imagination Library edition is published by Penguin Young Readers, a division of Penguin Random House, exclusively for Dolly Parton's Imagination Library, a not-for-profit program designed to inspire a love of reading and learning, sponsored in part by The Dollywood Foundation. Penguin's trade editions of this work are available wherever books are sold.